Flying Spider

Written by Jill Eggleton
Illustrated by Stella Yang

The spider went
under a leaf.
"I am looking for lunch,"
he said.

"Here comes a fly,"
said the spider.

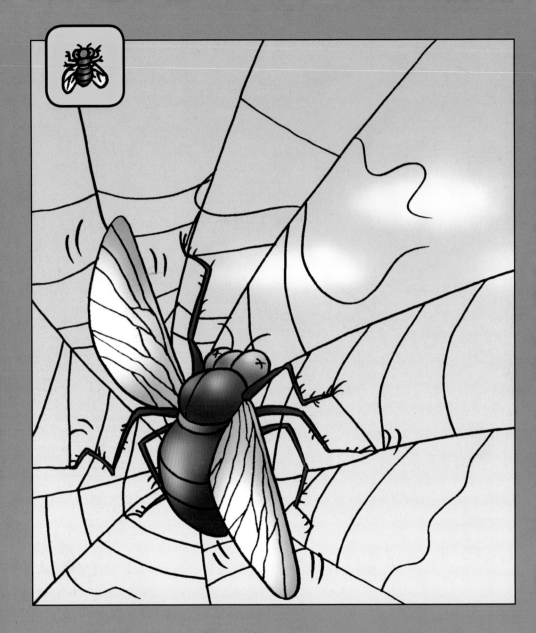

The fly went
into the web.

"**Yum**," said the spider.
"A fly for me."

A bee went
into the web.

"**Yum**," said the spider.
"A bee for me."

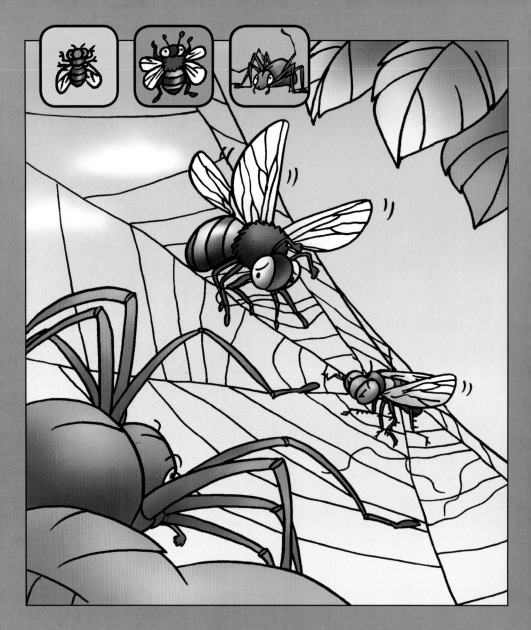

The spider went
into the web.

"Eeeek!" said the spider.
"Here comes a bird."

The web went
into the sky.
Whooosh!

10

"I can fly,"
said the fly.

"I can fly,"
said the bee.

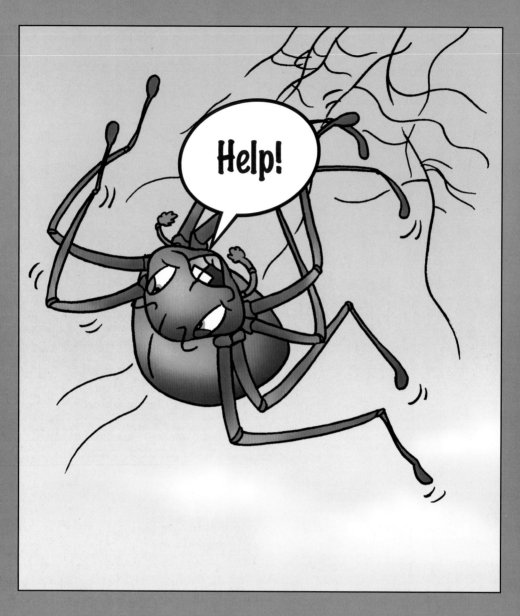

"**Help!**" said the spider.
"I can **not** fly."

The spider went . . .
down,
down,
down!

"Here comes a spider,"
said the lizard.
"**Yum!**"

A Flow Diagram

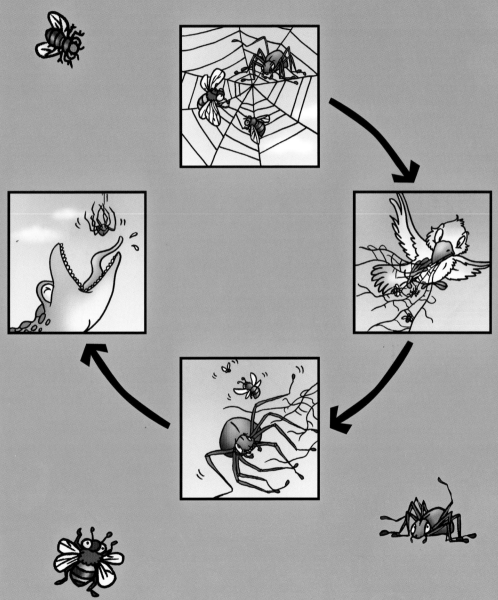

▬▬▬ **Guide Notes**

Title: Flying Spider
Stage: Early (1) – Red

Genre: Fiction
Approach: Guided Reading
Processes: Thinking Critically, Exploring Language, Processing Information
Written and Visual Focus: Flow Diagram, Cumulative Sequence Panels
Word Count: 103

THINKING CRITICALLY
(sample questions)
- What do you think this story could be about?
- Look at the title and read it to the children.
- Why do you think the fly and the bee went into the web?
- What do you think might have happened if the bird hadn't flown away with the web?
- How do you think the bee and the fly felt when the bird took the web?
- What do you think might have happened to the spider if the lizard hadn't been there?

EXPLORING LANGUAGE

Terminology
Title, cover, illustrations, author, illustrator

Vocabulary
Interest words: yum, eeeek, web, whooosh
High-frequency words: comes, looking
Positional words: down, under, into

Print Conventions
Capital letter for sentence beginnings and names, periods, commas, quotation marks
exclamation marks, ellipsis